PUFFIN BOOKS
The Day Grandfather Tickled a Tiger

Born in Kasauli in 1934, Ruskin Bond grew up in Jamnagar, Dehradun, New Delhi and Shimla. His first novel, *The Room on the Roof*, written when he was seventeen, received the John Llewellyn Rhys Memorial Prize in 1957. Since then he has written over five hundred short stories, essays and novellas (some included in the collections *Dust on the Mountain* and *Classic Ruskin Bond*) and more than forty books for children.

He received the Sahitya Akademi Award for English writing in India in 1993, the Padma Shri in 1999 and the Delhi government's Lifetime Achievement Award in 2012. He was awarded the Sahitya Akademi's Bal Sahitya Puraskar for his 'total contribution to children's literature' in 2013 and was honoured with the Padma Bhushan in 2014. He lives in Landour, Mussoorie, with his extended family.

ALSO IN PUFFIN BY RUSKIN BOND

RUSKIN BOND

The Day Grandfather Tickled a Tiger

Illustrations by
Viplov Singh

PUFFIN BOOKS
An imprint of Penguin Random House

PUFFIN BOOKS

USA | Canada | UK | Ireland | Australia
New Zealand | India | South Africa | China | Singapore

Penguin Books is part of the Penguin Random House group of companies
whose addresses can be found at global.penguinrandomhouse.com

Published by Penguin Random House India Pvt. Ltd
4th Floor, Capital Tower 1, MG Road,
Gurugram 122 002, Haryana, India

Penguin
Random House
India

First published in Puffin Books as part of *The Room of Many Colours*
by Penguin Books India 2001
This illustrated edition published 2017

Text copyright © Ruskin Bond 2001
Illustrations copyright © Viplov Singh 2017

This is a work of fiction. Names, characters, places and incidents are either the
product of the author's imagination or are used fictiously and any resemblance
to any actual person, living or dead, events or locales is entirely coincidental.

ISBN 9780143428732

Typeset in Sabon
Book design and layout by Devangana Dash
Printed at : Aarvee Promotions India

www.penguin.co.in

Chapter 1

TIMOTHY, THE TIGER CUB, was discovered by Grandfather on a hunting expedition in the Terai jungle near Dehra. Grandfather was no shikari, but as he knew the forests of the Siwalik hills better than most people, he was persuaded to accompany the party—it consisted of several Very Important Persons from Delhi—to advise on the terrain and the direction the beaters should take once a tiger had been spotted.

The camp itself was sumptuous—seven large tents (one for each shikari), a dining tent and a number of servants' tents. The dinner was very good, as Grandfather admitted afterwards; it was not often that one saw hot-water plates, finger-glasses and seven or eight courses in a tent in the jungle! But that was how things were done in the days of the Viceroys . . . There were also some fifteen elephants, four of them with howdahs for the shikaris, and the others specially trained for taking part in the beat.

The sportsmen never saw a tiger, nor did they shoot anything else, though they saw a number of deer, peacock and wild boar.

They were giving up all hope of finding a tiger and were beginning to shoot at jackals, when Grandfather, strolling down the forest path at some distance from the rest of the party, discovered a little tiger about eighteen inches long, hiding among the intricate roots of a banyan tree.

Grandfather picked him up and brought him home after the camp had broken up. He had the distinction of being the only member of the party to have bagged any game, dead or alive.

Chapter 2

At first the tiger cub, who was named Timothy by Grandmother, was brought up entirely on milk given to him in a feeding bottle by our cook, Mahmoud. But the milk proved too rich for him, and he was put on a diet of raw mutton and cod liver oil, to be followed later by a more tempting diet of pigeons and rabbits.

Timothy was provided with two companions—Toto the monkey, who was bold enough to pull the young tiger by the tail and then climb up the curtains if Timothy lost his temper; and

a small mongrel puppy, found on the road by Grandfather. At first Timothy appeared to be quite afraid of the puppy, and darted back with a spring if it came too near.

He would make absurd dashes at it with his large forepaws and then retreat to a ridiculously safe distance.

Finally, he allowed the puppy to crawl on his back and rest there! One of Timothy's favourite amusements was to stalk anyone who would play with him, and so, when I came to live with Grandfather, I became one of the tiger's favourites. With a crafty look in his glittering eyes, and his body crouching, he would creep closer and closer to me, suddenly making a dash for my feet, rolling over on his back and kicking with delight, and pretending to bite my ankles.

He was by this time the size of a full-grown retriever, and when I took him out for walks, people on the road would give us a wide berth. When he pulled hard on his chain, I had difficulty keeping up with him. His favourite place in the house was the drawing room, and he would make himself comfortable on the long sofa, reclining there with great dignity, and snarling at anybody who tried to get him off.

Chapter 3

Timothy had clean habits, and would scrub his face with his paws exactly like a cat. He slept at night in the cook's quarters, and was always delighted at being let out by him in the morning.

'One of these days,' declared Grandmother in her prophetic manner, 'we are going to find Timothy sitting on Mahmoud's bed, and no sign of the cook except his clothes and shoes!'

Of course, it never came to that, but when Timothy was about six months old a change came over him; he grew steadily less friendly. When out for a walk with me, he would try to steal away to stalk a cat or someone's pet Pekinese. Sometimes at night we would hear frenzied cackling from the poultry house, and in the morning there would be feathers lying all over the veranda.

Timothy had to be chained up more often. And, finally, when he began to stalk Mahmoud about the house with what looked like villainous intent, Grandfather decided it was time to transfer him to a zoo.

The nearest zoo was at Lucknow, two hundred miles away. Reserving a first-class compartment for himself and Timothy—no one would share a compartment with them—Grandfather took him to Lucknow, where the zoo authorities were only too glad to receive as a gift a well-fed and fairly civilized tiger.

About six months later, when my grandparents were visiting relatives in Lucknow, Grandfather took the opportunity of calling at the zoo to see how Timothy was getting on. I was not there to accompany him, but I heard all about it when he returned to Dehra.

Arriving at the zoo, Grandfather made straight for the particular cage in which Timothy had been interned. The tiger was there, crouched in a corner, full-grown and with a magnificent striped coat.

'Hello Timothy!' said Grandfather and, climbing the railing with ease, put his arm through the bars of the cage.

The tiger approached the bars, and allowed Grandfather to put both hands around his head. Grandfather stroked the tiger's forehead and tickled his ear, and, whenever he growled, smacked him across the mouth, which was his old way of keeping him quiet.

Chapter 4

He licked Grandfather's hands and only sprang away when a leopard in the next cage snarled at him.

Grandfather 'shooed' the leopard away, and the tiger returned to lick his hands; but every now and then the leopard would rush at the bars, and the tiger would slink back to his corner.

A number of people had gathered to watch the reunion when a keeper pushed his way through the crowd and asked Grandfather what he was doing.

'I'm talking to Timothy,' said Grandfather. 'Weren't you here when I gave him to the zoo six months ago?'

'I haven't been here very long,' said the surprised keeper. 'Please continue your conversation. But I have never been able to touch him myself, he is always very bad tempered.'

Grandfather had been stroking and slapping Timothy for about five minutes when he found another keeper observing him with some alarm. He recognized him as the keeper who had been there when Timothy had first come to the zoo.

'You remember me,' said Grandfather. 'Now why don't you transfer Timothy to another cage, away from this stupid leopard?'

'But—sir—' stammered the keeper, 'it is not your tiger.'

'I know, I know,' said Grandfather testily. 'I realize he is no longer mine. But you might at least take a suggestion or two from me.'

'I remember your tiger very well,' said the keeper. 'He died two months ago.'

'Died!' exclaimed Grandfather.

'Yes, sir, of pneumonia. This tiger was trapped in the hills only last month, and he is very dangerous!'

Grandfather could think of nothing to say. The tiger was still licking his arm, with increasing relish. Grandfather took what seemed to him an age to withdraw his hand from the cage. With his face near the tiger's he mumbled, 'Goodnight, Timothy,' and, giving the keeper a scornful look, walked briskly out of the zoo.

More in the series by Ruskin Bond

Everything that you've always loved about Ruskin Bond is back. His mesmerizing descriptions of nature and his wonderful way with words—this is Ruskin Bond at his finest.

Read on as Rusty tells the story of his grandfather's relationship with the trees around him, who's convinced that they love him back with as much tenderness as he loves them.

Ranji's team finds an unexpected opponent— a nosy crocodile—when they play a cricket match against the village boys. Annoyed at the swarms of boys crowding the riverbank and the alarming cricket balls plopping around his place of rest, Nakoo the crocodile decides to take his revenge.

Bisnu finds how dangerous and lonely life can be for a boy who has to leave his home to earn money for his family. As he sets to work on the limestone quarries with the choking dust enveloping the beautiful mountain air, he longs for home more than ever.

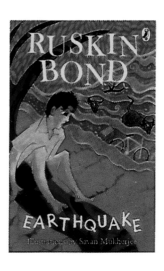

'What do you do when there's an earthquake?' asks Rakesh. Everyone in the Burman household has their own ideas, but when the tremors begin, they are all taken by surprise. Amidst the destruction, Rakesh's family stays strong. But will they survive the onslaught of yet another earthquake?